PAISLEY THE PONY

AN ASSATEAGUE ISLAND ADVENTURE

By Cindy Freland

This book is dedicated to my beautiful daughters,
Andrea and Alyssa Bean,
and my dear friend, Chris Hahn,
a Kansas Delaware Native American

Thanks for all the encouragement,
love and laughter. I love you!

Never in my wildest dreams could I ever imagine there was a herd of ponies living on a beach. I had heard of wild horses in movies taking place in Nevada and Colorado and other western parts of the United States, but never on the Eastern Shore of Maryland.

Alyssa loved visiting Assateague Island. She visited the ponies, swam, she went crabbing, fishing, and boating, and watched for any of the 320 species of birds. She traveled to spectacular natural settings where wild ponies, birds, dolphins, and majestic bald eagles were seen along with the Assateague Lighthouse.

If this sounds like a dream, it surely was to her. She loved being outside and especially on the island seeing all the wonderful animals.

Her grandparents first brought her there in 1890, when she was only ten years old. Now that she had grandchildren of her own, she

enjoyed the beauty and solitude of the island and she told her grandchildren stories of the wild ponies that graced the seashores.

Alyssa and her six-year-old granddaughter, Savannah, loved snuggling up in the big, comfy chair by the fireplace in the old farmhouse. The living room walls were covered in photos of American Indians and horses.

"Grandma, will you please tell me the story of Paisley the Pony?" asked Savannah.

"Of course! I remember one story that my great-grandmother told about the 56-canon Spanish warship, La Galga, Spanish for "the greyhound." It was heading towards Spain, 4,650 miles across the Atlantic Ocean, but wrecked near Assateague Island after a fierce hurricane knocked it 1,000 miles off course in 1750," Alyssa started.

One of the ponies that survived that terrible storm was a gorgeous brown and white filly, or young female pony. Her name was Paisley because of the white paisley, or teardrop, shape on her side. Paisley and 26 of her friends swam to the beach.

The 200 crew members swam to the island and they got help from the American Indians to get the cargo ashore. **The Indians taught the ship's crew how to plant corn, beans, and squash, as well as where to find clams and oysters.** The ship's crew, the Indians, and the ponies lived on the island peacefully.

Paisley and her friends enjoyed lying in the warm sand to rest and dried off after their long swim from the ship.

"Poet, do you think we will have to get back on that ship again?" asked Paisley.

"I sure hope not, Paisley. I didn't care much for being tied up in the cramped stalls, with the musty hay, and I was always hungry," said Poet.

"Grandma, did the ponies really talk?"

"That is the way I heard the story, Savannah."

The Algonquin Indian tribe that lived on the island had never seen horses until then. When they discovered the man was riding on the back of the horse, they were amazed at the strength and power of those beautiful animals. People of the tribe learned to ride the horses very quickly and use them to make work easier.

Paisley was given as the eighth birthday present to Kanti, by her father, the chief of the tribe. Kanti and Paisley worked hard and

had great fun together. They helped the tribe by carrying firewood, water, and crops. Paisley was more of a precious companion than a work horse so she never had to plow the fields or carry anything too heavy. She was even permitted to roam free and she frequently visited the other ponies on the island.

When Paisley visited her friends, she liked visiting her best friend, Poet. He was her age, about the same size, and they were side-by-side on the ship. They even helped each other get free from the sinking ship and swam to shore together.

It started raining hard so Paisley and Poet found a cave to stay warm and dry. They talked about the terrible conditions on the ship and all the great adventures they would have on the island.

"Look, Poet, the water is landing in that hole. We will have fresh water to drink here every time the sky falls," said Paisley.

There was so much work that needed to be done before winter. But Kanti was tired of working and she wanted to have a little fun. When Paisley returned Kanti jumped on her back and rode to the beach as fast as she could. At first they walked slowly in the warm sand and enjoyed the spray from the bay. Then they galloped along the water's edge and splashed water all over themselves. It was hours before they returned as they really enjoyed the fresh, clean air, golden beach, shimmering water, and each other's company.

When they got back, Kanti's mother asked her to start making a basket. Even though Kanti was tired from her ride along the beach, she did what her mother asked. Baskets were made by women to hold bread, fruits, clothes, and sewing. The baskets were also traded for other things that were needed. They made baskets from

many things but their favorite was sweetgrass as it was softer and smelled like fresh hay. Kanti worked on the basket using a bone needle and basswood fiber to connect the sweetgrass coils while Paisley explored the beach with her friends.

"Paisley, what do you like eating most on the island," asked Poet.
"I love the cord grass but it is very salty. I have to drink lots of water to balance the salt," said Paisley.

When Kanti had enough of basket making, she went to find Paisley. Paisley was Kanti's precious companion and she wanted to be sure she was okay before going to bed. Kanti walked along the beach and saw Paisley gracefully prancing in the moonlight with her friends.

"Poet, what are you doing?" asked Paisley.

"I just love prancing in the moonlight with my friends. The sand tickles my feet," said Poet.

Paisley pranced in the moonlight with Poet and found that it was enchanting.

The next day Paisley and her friends searched for bayberry twigs, marsh and sand dune grasses, persimmons, and rosehips. They also ate the salt marsh cordgrass along Assateague Island's shoreline. The ponies got rid of the flies by spending a lot of time in the surf, letting the breezes carry away the flying pests. They had to stay strong and healthy as they were very important to the tribe.

Some of the horses were trained as bison horses and were prized among warriors. They ran alongside bison during a hunt. Without these specially trained horses, it was hard for warriors to provide enough food for their families. The highly prized horses were kept inside the lodge at night or a nearby corral.

As Kanti and Paisley grew older, they did more and more together. Over their many years together, they established a great love and respect for each other. Kanti and Paisley were best friends.

When Kanti was 16 she wanted to enter the Great Pony Race. But only men were permitted to race and they ran the entire 37 mile length of the beach and back. Algonquin Indians from all over Maryland entered the race to see which rider was fastest.

Kanti's friend, Mingan, was already entered in the race but he didn't have a pony. His pony was stolen a few months ago and he never found him. Kanti offered to let Mingan ride Paisley in the race as long as he could control her. But that would be a great challenge as Paisley had never been ridden by anyone but Kanti.

Mingan tried and tried to get Paisley to like him and allow him to get on her back. But Paisley was only used to Kanti riding her and she just wouldn't have anyone else.

He tried again but Paisley was scared and ran off. She ran and ran until she was out of sight. Paisley found a cave and hid overnight.

Kanti and Mingan found Paisley in the cave the next morning. To their amazement, Paisley was friendly to Mingan.

They found interesting drawings on the cave walls that showed ponies crossing a narrow inlet. But what did the drawings mean?

"This is where they got the idea for the pony penning that started in 1925," Alyssa told Savannah.

"What is the pony penning, Grandma?" Savannah asked.

"I will tell you after I finish the story of Paisley the Pony," said Alyssa.

When they got back to the village, Paisley permitted Mingan to ride her. Now was the time to practice for the race. First they walked fast, then they ran slowly, then they ran fast. They ran the entire length of the beach and back. They practiced every day for the next three weeks.

The exciting day of the race was finally here. Kanti and Mingan were so excited that it made Paisley nervous. Paisley didn't seem well at all. Practicing hard for three weeks had made her sick but no one noticed.

The riders were lined up on the beach to start racing. The Chief signaled for them to start running. They took off like the speed of light.

Mingan and Paisley started out very quickly and were ahead. But then half way to the end of the beach, Paisley felt sick and slowed down. Then she stopped. Mingan was angry and wondered why Paisley would stop in the middle of the race. She was prepared for this. They trained for three long weeks and Paisley was a strong pony.

Poet ran by with Huritt and noticed Paisley had stopped running. Poet was concerned for his friend. Mingan jumped off Paisley and she collapsed into the sand.

"Oh, no, Grandma, was Paisley okay?"

Poet and Huritt saw what happened and they ran back to check it out. Paisley was still lying in the sand and breathing heavily. Huritt invited Mingan to jump onto Poet so they could ride back to the village together. Kanti needed to know that Paisley was sick.

With her father's permission, Kanti and Mingan jumped on her father's horse, Chepi, and they rode with Poet and Huritt to Paisley.

"What's wrong, Paisley?" asked Poet.

"I am not sure, Poet. But my legs hurt really badly," said Paisley.

Kanti realized that her beloved companion was in a lot of pain. So she asked Mingan and Huritt to find a prickly pear cactus and bring back a pad from the cactus, and a fruit, called tuna. She told them to be very careful with the spines on the cactus. They raced off on Chepi and found the cactus.

"What? The fruit is called tuna?" asked Savannah.

They noticed the long spines on the pads and tunas so they used a rock to break them off the cactus. Then they broke off the spines

from the pad and tunas. They put them into the bag that Kanti had made from a deer skin.

They raced back to help Paisley after gathering the tunas. After rubbing the fruit on Paisley's legs, she began to feel much better. In a few hours, she was back on her feet and they all went back to the village.

Mingan felt badly for riding Paisley after weeks of training and no rest. He told Kanti he was sorry for training and riding Paisley so hard. They will have to wait until next year to try the race again.

When Kanti got back to her village she told her mother that Paisley collapsed during the race and how Mingan brought back the tunas and rubbed them on Paisley's legs. But she also remembered that she found the drawings in the cave and asked her mother to go see them with her.

When Kanti and her mother went into the cave, they discovered more hallways to explore. The cave ceiling was covered with bats and there were spiders and crickets crawling on the floor. Small fish were in the shimmering pools of fresh water.

There were many pools of fresh water for drinking and the temperature was cool enough for food storage. They would have to build storage boxes so the animals wouldn't eat the food. But the cave would keep it cold through the hot summers.

They found each wall was covered in drawings of Indians, horses, and an inlet not too far from their village. This made them curious as to why the horses were in the water in the cave drawing and where the inlet was located.

After a few weeks Paisley was much better. Kanti rode Paisley and Kanti's mother rode her horse and several other people of the

village traveled to the inlet.

They found other villages beyond the inlet with which to trade horses, beads, and furs. The water was very shallow and it would be a great way to get the horses across for trading.

"They didn't know it at the time but that began the pony penning we know today," said Alyssa.

"What is pony penning, Grandma?" asked Savannah.

"Pony penning has been a great tradition since 1925 when the "Saltwater Cowboys" round up 150 adult horses and 70 foals. The cowboys herd the horses from the beach on Assateague Island through the inlet and onto the beach on Chincoteague, Virginia.

There are thousands of spectators and lots of festivals around the pony penning each year. Visitors can even take a boat from Ocean City, Maryland, to Assateague Island to see the ponies in their natural habitat. They also learn about the lighthouse and other creatures of the island, including horseshoe crabs, bald eagles, and dolphins."

"That sounds wonderful and I would love to see the island, the lighthouse, and all the wild horses, Grandma. Why do you love them so much and why do you have all these photos on your walls?"

"I am so glad you asked about the photos, Savannah. I love the wild ponies and the American Indians of Assateague Island because they are stories passed down through our Algonquin ancestors. One of your ancestors was Kanti and she loved Paisley the Pony. I hope you will enjoy the island and love the ponies as much as I do."

THE END

FACTS ABOUT THE WILD PONIES

1. The Chincoteague Pony, or the Assateague horse, is a breed of pony that lives in a feral condition, or in the wild, in Virginia and Maryland.
2. The wild ponies have been roaming Assateague Island since 1750 when a Spanish ship carrying the horses wrecked there during a hurricane.
3. They eat bayberry twigs, marsh and sand dune grasses, persimmons, and rosehips. They also eat the salt marsh cordgrass along Assateague Island's shoreline.
4. The ponies are much smaller than other horses. They eat salt grasses and the salt makes their bellies rounder.
5. The ponies get rid of flies by spending a lot of time in the surf, letting the breezes carry away the flying pests.
6. Pony penning started in 1835, with town residents rounding up ponies on horseback and removing some of them to the mainland. In 1924 the first "Pony Penning Day" was held by the Chincoteague Volunteer Fire Company, where ponies were auctioned to raise money for fire trucks. The annual event has continued in the same way each July.

BOOKS WRITTEN
BY CINDY FRELAND

You will find the following children's books written by Cindy Freland on Amazon.com:

Jordan the Jellyfish: A Chesapeake Bay Adventure
Curtis the Crab: A Chesapeake Bay Adventure
Heather the Honey Bee: A Chesapeake Bay Adventure
Oakley the Oyster: A Chesapeake Bay Adventure
Olivia the Osprey: A Chesapeake Bay Adventure
Chester the Chipmunk: A Chesapeake Bay Adventure
Christmas with Marco: A Chesapeake Bay Adventure
Lila the Ladybug: A Deep Creek Lake Adventure
Vandi the Garden Fairy
Mud Pies

Also please check out www.cbaykidsbooks.com.

Author: Cindy Freland

Cindy Freland's inspiration comes from her love of children and animals. Most of her children's books are based on true events. She worked for a major health insurance company for 25 years, founded and managed a secretarial business starting in 1997, and is now an Aide at a private school. Her books are available in 46 retail locations in Maryland, Virginia, and New York and 24 libraries in Maryland. You can find her books on www.cbaykidsbooks.com and www.amazon.com. Freland lives in Bowie, Maryland, with her family and dog, Juno.

Illustrator:
Emily Hercock

I am a freelance illustrator based in a small village in Norfolk, UK and have illustrated over 20 books in my three year career. I work from my home where I live with my wonderful husband and Dougal, my cat, who keeps me company as I work.

I began drawing as soon as I could hold a pen and now at age 25 I am proud to run my own business, "Emily's illustrations," doing what I love as a career.

I left school at age 17 with top grades in GCSE art but was unable to go on to further education due to family circumstances. I went straight to work at various retail stores where I would always be doodling on the back of receipts!

I was married in 2014 to my husband, Michael Hercock, who has supported me in starting and growing my business. I doubt I would be where I am now without his encouragement and belief in me and my work.

I became ill in 2015 with Chronic Fatigue Syndrome and had to give up working as a cleaner. I was determined to continue to work and whilst scrolling through a chat room for authors (where I was looking for advice on a book I was trying to write) I found a lady looking for an illustrator. I applied and that was the beginning of my career.

Now in year three of my career in illustration and I have had the privilege to work with Cindy Freland and her wonderful series of children's books about the Chesapeake Bay area. Illustrating her book "Paisley the Pony" has been nothing short of a delight.

My business continues to grow and I continue to love illustrating for the world's children.

You can find my website at: http: www.emily-jade-illustrator.com.

CPSIA information can be obtained
at www.ICGtesting.com
Printed in the USA
LVIC06n1731160517
534740LV00002B/16

* 9 7 8 1 9 4 1 9 2 7 9 4 6 *